SO-AKN-075

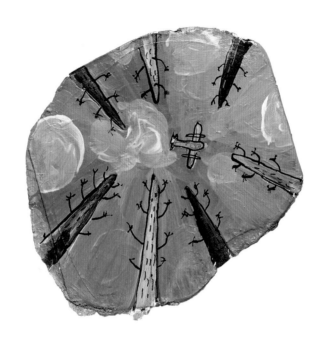

FOR MIKE. AND SHANNON, CAITIE, ALLIE AND JAKE. xoxo —LC

FOR REBECCA AND NOBLE. —MJ

Text copyright © 2010 by Laurel Croza
Illustrations copyright © 2010 by Matt James
First published in Canada and the USA in 2010 by Groundwood Books
Thirty-fifth anniversary edition published in 2013

All rights reserved. No part of this publication may be reproduced, stored in a retrieval system or transmitted, in any form or by any means, without the prior written consent of the publisher or a license from The Canadian Copyright Licensing Agency (Access Copyright). For an Access Copyright license, visit www.accesscopyright.ca or call toll free to 1-800-893-5777.

Groundwood Books / House of Anansi Press
110 Spadina Avenue, Suite 801, Toronto, Ontario M5V 2K4
or c/o Publishers Group West
1700 Fourth Street, Berkeley, CA 94710

We acknowledge for their financial support of our publishing program the Canada Council for the Arts, the Government of Canada through the Canada Book Fund (CBF) and the Ontario Arts Council.

 Canada Council Conseil des Arts
for the Arts du Canada

 ONTARIO ARTS COUNCIL
CONSEIL DES ARTS DE L'ONTARIO

Library and Archives Canada Cataloguing in Publication
Croza, Laurel
I know here / Laurel Croza ; pictures by Matt James.
Issued also in an electronic format.
ISBN 978-1-55498-393-3
I. James, Matt II. Title.
PS8605.R698I4 2013   jC813'.6   C2013-901079-3

The illustrations were done in acrylic and India ink on panel.
Design by Michael Solomon
Printed and bound in China

ROZA,

I KNOW HERE

Laurel Croza   PICTURES BY Matt James

Groundwood Books   House of Anansi Press   Toronto   Berkeley

CAROL STREAM PUBLIC LIBRARY

0/14

DOUG runs down the steps of our trailer. He's bursting with news.

"We're moving," he shouts. "We're moving to Toronto. When summer comes."

Our friends circle around him.

The dam our dad is building is almost finished. By summer it will send out electricity far across the prairies. Soon we will all be leaving.

I follow my brother, kicking the packed dirt. Swirls of dust puff up and turn my rubber boots gray.

This is where I live. I don't know Toronto.
I know here.

I know this road, the one I am walking on. One end goes to the dam and the other end stops at my school. I count the trailers on my side of the road. There are seven and mine makes eight.

I know the forest behind my home where I play hide-and-seek in and out of the pine trees, the needles soft like a quilt under my feet. I know the howling sound a wolf makes when it calls out at night in that very same forest.

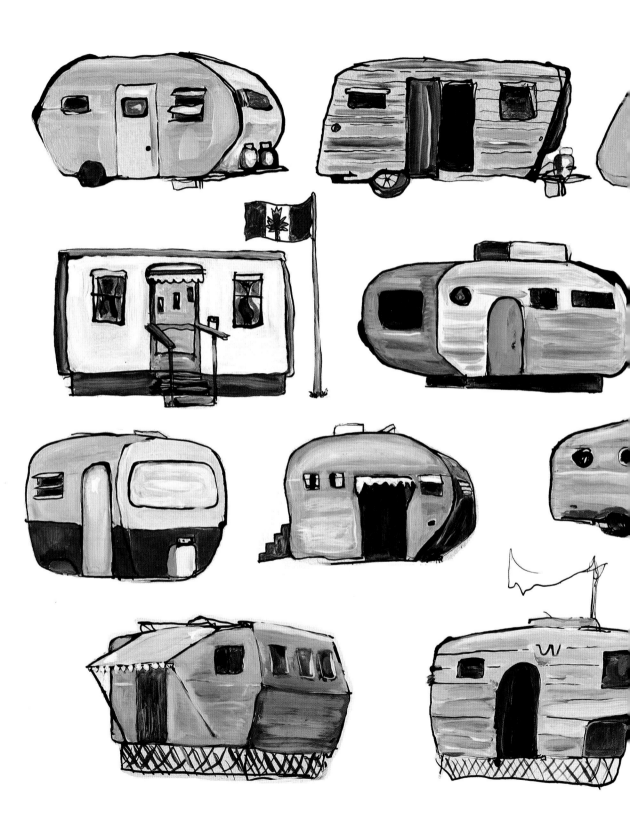

I count the trailers on the other side of the road. There are ten. A fox lives in a cage behind one of them. I know the fox's damp fur smell before I see him.

I know the hill behind those trailers. It's a good tobogganing hill when it snows. And I know the creek that winds around behind that hill. And the squishy spot by the beaver dam where my little sister, Kathie, catches frogs and puts them in a bucket.

I know the truck that is driving towards me,
bits of gravel jumping up and dancing under
the tires. The man inside the truck waves at
me. He is stopping at each trailer to deliver
groceries.

Our school is the trailer at the end of the road.
Miss Hendrickson, our teacher, is standing
on the wooden steps waiting for me. I know
everyone in my school. I count nine of us, three
rows of desks. Only me in grade three.

Doug is in grade four. He asks Miss Hendrickson to show us where Toronto is. She turns to the map of Canada hanging on the wall behind her desk. First she points to where we are. Miss Hendrickson has made a yellow dot to mark where we live. She has made a blue line for the dam, built right across the North Saskatchewan River. There is Carrot River where Michael, my baby brother, was born, and there is Nipawin where our groceries come from. Miss Hendrickson moves her finger along the map, out of Saskatchewan, past Manitoba. She stops in Ontario.

"Here is Toronto, the city of Toronto," she says. There is a big red star beside it on the map.

I sit in my desk and
look at that star and I ask
Miss Hendrickson, "Have
people in Toronto seen
what I've seen?"

I have seen an old moose standing still in the water, looking straight at me. Rabbits and deer running beside my dad's truck on the Pas Trail. A forest fire across the river, the tops of the trees popping and shooting flames, sparks landing on my side of the shore.

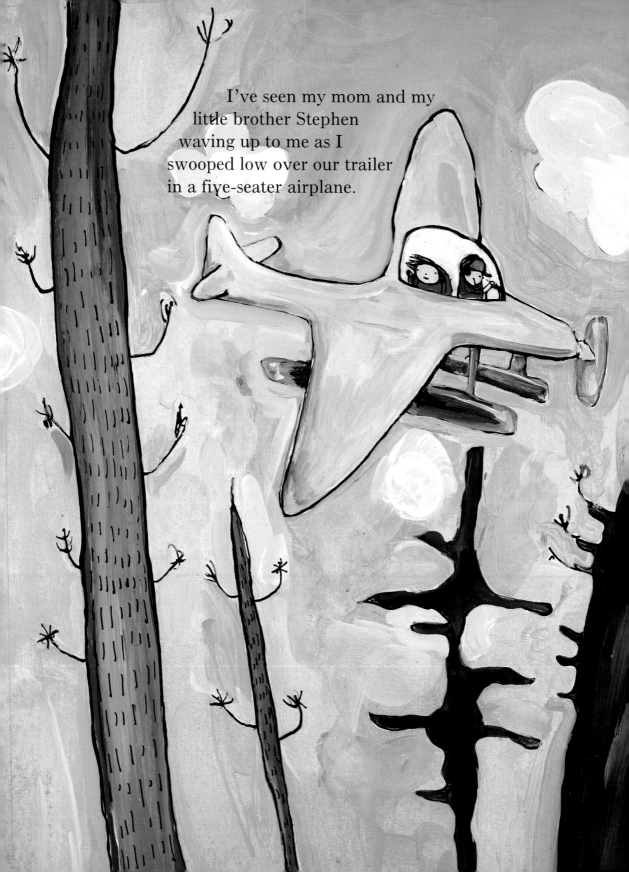

I've seen my mom and my little brother Stephen waving up to me as I swooped low over our trailer in a five-seater airplane.

One Sunday night I saw *The Wonderful World of Disney* on a TV that the electrician set up outside his trailer.

Miss Hendrickson says that after lunch we will draw a picture, a picture of something we have seen, something we want to remember, to take with us when we leave.

I follow Doug and our friends as they run back down the road. I see Kathie waiting for me in front of our trailer, with her bucket of frogs. I look further down the road where it disappears through the trees on its way to the dam. I see my dad in his truck, driving home to eat lunch with us.

And I know what I will do.

I will draw this road, my road. I will draw the trailers and the forest and the hill and the creek and the beaver dam.

I will show my picture to Miss Hendrickson, and then I'll fold it up. I will fold up the howl of the wolf and the smell of the fox in his cage and the stare of the old moose and the feel of my heart beating fast as I swooped over my road in a five-seater airplane. I will fold my drawing up small, put it safe in my pocket and I will take my road with me. To Toronto. As soon as summer comes.

This is what I know. Here.

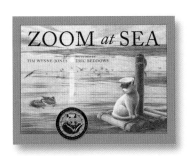

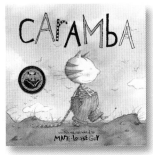

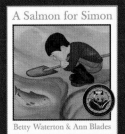

SASKATCHEWAN

C A N

MANITOBA

Nipawin

Carrol River

TOBA

UNITED STATES